A Foxfield R[...]

Bel and the kittens

STORY BY **Richmond Warner**

ILLUSTRATIONS BY **Sarah-Leigh Wills**

Bel and the Kittens

Typeset in New Century Schoolbook LT Std

Illustrations by Sarah-Leigh Wills, photographs © B Elms

Editing, design, typesetting and publishing by UK Book Publishing
www.ukbookpublishing.com

ISBN: 978-1-912183-23-4

www.foxfieldrailway.co.uk

photo © B Elms

Bellerophon, the "Kittens", Barney, Sam, Samantha and Ee'boo at the Foxfield Railway in May 2017.

www.foxfieldrailway.co.uk

Mr Barnabas Pyke is on Facebook! You can keep up to date with him and learn about other Foxfield Railway stories by visiting Barnabas Pyke on

www.facebook.com

Author's Note

'Bel and the Kittens' is set in Staffordshire in the 1950s telling the story of two young children, Sam and Samantha, and their adventures on the Foxfield Railway and in Highwayman's Wood.

The world was very different then. Few people had telephones or TVs or cars and almost everything was coal-powered. It seems a very long time ago but your grandparents will remember it well if you ask them.

But the places described in this book – the railway, the wood, the colliery – still exist today. You can visit them on the Foxfield Steam Railway near Stoke-on-Trent. You are welcome to visit, meet Barney and Ee'boo and even ride on Bel and the Kittens.

Chapter 1

"A wasted journey," grumbled Sam. Sam and Samantha had come to Highwayman's Wood to see the baby rabbits and the baby ducklings on the pond, but there were none. However, Sam was wrong about a wasted journey. For at that very moment something caught his eye. Something that was different.

At first he was not at all sure what it was. Beyond the grassy bank, just past where the meadow met the wood, there was an old water tower beside the railway line. It had been built many years ago to provide water for the steam locomotives. A large, metal circular tank on top of a very tall iron column. It was rusty – like so much else on the railway – and had not been used for many years. Leading from the ground to the top of the tower, where an old chain dangled down from the top of the tank, was a rickety old ladder. Today, near the top of the ladder something was sitting...something the children had never seen before...

"Look!" said Sam. "Look there on the tower!"

"I know – I can see – what on earth is it?" said Samantha.

The two children slowly walked to the edge of the wood, to get a better view. Sitting near the top of the ladder, looking back at them through eyes as big as saucers, was quite simply the most enormous owl they had ever seen. The children slowly and quietly walked right up to the tower, trying not to frighten the owl. They stood and stared at the owl, fascinated. The owl stared back at them. But whether the owl was as fascinated by the children as they were with him was impossible to say. For this was an owl whose expression gave nothing away.

"That's a very big owl," whispered Samantha.

"A very big owl," her brother agreed.

"I've never seen an owl here before. I thought they only came out at night."

The twins stood for a long time in silence, totally captivated by the beautiful creature, as is always the case with owls. The children continued to gaze at the owl and the owl continued to gaze back at the children. He didn't seem at all concerned by his two admirers.

"Only come out at night... Really, the sheer ignorance of it all," said the owl.

An astonished Sam and Samantha turned and looked at each other, open mouthed.

"Did you hear....? ...I thought..." said Samantha.

"I don't know..." Sam replied, unsure, not knowing if he was imagining things.

"It's rude to ignore someone who speaks to you. Especially when you're staring at them. Don't you know that?" said the owl. "You might at least have wished me Good Morning."

"Good... good morning," said Samantha.

"Yes, er... hello," said Sam.

"And Good Morning to you, too," the owl replied, bowing his head slightly. "Did I hear you say you were looking for baby rabbits? Did you find any?"

"No, there were none," said Samantha.

"Pity," sighed the owl. "I do like baby rabbits."

"You must have very good hearing if you heard us say that when we were right over there," said Samantha.

"Owls have the best hearing of any creature.

Don't you know that? Actually, owls are best at most things."

"I didn't know that," admitted Sam. "And I didn't know that owls can talk either. Or that they come out during the day."

"Oh yes. Owls can, well, can do almost anything, really. But we rarely talk in front of people. That is generally not a wise thing to do."

"There's a parrot in the pet shop in Longton who can talk," Sam remembered.

"Parrots, really!" The owl shook his head dismissively. "Such silly creatures. All gossip and fancy feathers."

"We've not seen you here before. Have you just come?" asked Samantha.

"I came here three days ago."

"Why?" asked Sam.

"Why not?" the owl replied. "I often come here, should I choose to. I've been coming here since long before you two were born. I might also ask you – why did you come here?"

"Well, we came here... because we wanted to..." said Samantha.

"And so did I," said the owl, sniffily. "And I do rather like this old water tower. It's nice and high off the ground. It's got a wooden cover on top of the tank to keep the rain out. It's got sides all round to keep off the wind. It's got a pipe inside which is perfect to perch on. A panel has fallen out – just here – so I can nip in and out just as I please. Goodbye." With that, and with a single flap of his huge wings, the owl went through the gap left by the missing panel and disappeared inside the water tank.

"He's gone," said Sam, disappointed.

"Yes, I can see that," said his sister.

"Should I climb up the ladder and see if I can find him in there?"

"No – you mustn't!" Samantha scolded him. She pointed to the sign on the ladder which read "DANGER DO NOT ENTER".

"It's dangerous to go up the ladder. The sign says so. It's old and rusty. It might break. You'd fall off and hurt yourself."

"I wonder when he'll come out again. I hope we'll see him again."

Samantha gave a deep sigh. "So do I."

Chapter 2

S am and Samantha loved coming to
Highwayman's Wood any time of year, but
especially now, in the springtime. It was Sunday
morning and the sun shone brightly, though the two
children were pleasantly shaded by the branches of
the trees reaching high above their heads.

Of course, the first thing they had done was race
to the old water tower to see if the owl was there.
The twins' hearts sank when he wasn't. They had
called and shouted to him, thinking he might be
asleep inside. But nothing. So, disappointed, the
children walked back into the wood and were
cheered up, a little, by finding a mother duck with
her ducklings on the pond.

Samantha was captivated by the carpet of bluebells all around. Last week when she and her brother had come to the wood the bluebells had still not woken from their winter sleep. But today the forest floor was the most wonderful, soft, gentle shade of blue. After watching the ducks – and finding the first baby rabbit of the year too – the children lay down for a while on a bank of soft moss and bracken.

"They're so beautiful – the bluebells!" Samantha said to her brother. "You can smell them too, such a warm, lovely scent."

But Sam was more interested in listening for the distant whistle which meant the steam train was approaching the level crossing at Cresswell Ford. And then he heard it!

"Come on," Sam said. "Or we'll miss seeing the train."

The two children scrambled to their feet and ran out of the wood to the wooden fence at the edge of the wood. Along the way was an old tree stump standing on its own in the grass. Sam leapt up on to it and stood there hoping to get a better look. Then he jumped off and joined his sister at the fence. Behind the fence ran the single track railway line linking the Foxfield colliery to the main railway line, taking wagons laden with coal from the mine to the factories, steelworks and potteries of Staffordshire.

Sam and Samantha clung onto the wooden fence. The wood felt warm from the sunshine. They always waited at this very place, right beside the big red signal, because when the signal was level it meant the train had to stop. The same line ran right behind the back garden of Grandmother's little cottage but the train never stopped there. However, when the train stopped here they could have a good look at the engine. A fascinating machine, Sam thought, and often the driver would have a few words with them. But the signal was pointing down today. This meant that the train wouldn't stop but would chug straight past.

"I can hear it!" shouted an excited Sam. "I hope it's Florence!" Florence was Sam's favourite engine. Six wheels and a wide chimney, the engine was painted a rich red colour, with all the brasswork polished till it glistened. Looking to their right the children saw the engine come into view, steam and smoke chuff-chuffing from the chimney.

"It is Florence!" said Sam. "I hope Barney's driving!" The neat little engine went past them pulling empty coal wagons back to the colliery. The two children waved excitedly. Barney was indeed

driving. He knew the children would be there on a
Sunday morning and he always looked out for them.
As the train approached Barney blew a "toot! toot!"
on Florence's whistle. He leaned out of the cab, raised
his bowler hat to the children and waved.

"Now then, me old ducks!" said Barney. The
children waved back. Barney was the children's
favourite driver. He was always cheery. He had
bushy white mutton-chop whiskers and wire-framed
spectacles perched on the end of his nose. He always
wore an old bowler hat, a black waistcoat and a red,
spotted handkerchief tied around his neck. Barney
had promised the twins that – when they were a
bit bigger – he would take them for a ride on the
locomotive, in the cab, all the way from the colliery
to the signal box at Blythe Bridge on the main line.
Sam couldn't wait! He would be ten in a few weeks'
time – surely that would be big enough?

Sam counted the empty wagons as they clanged
and jiggled behind the engine on the way back to
the colliery. There were six of them, large metal
tubs. There were always six, never more, never fewer.
Though Florence was always spotlessly clean and
polished the wagons were filthy with coal dust and
rust. If I were in charge of the railway, Samantha
thought to herself, I would give them a jolly good

wash. Sam and Samantha continued to watch the little train till it passed out of sight down the bank towards the colliery. Eventually the chuffing, chugging, clattering and banging were all gone. All was quiet again apart from the sound of the birds singing.

"What shall we do now?" Sam gave a big sigh. "It will be ages before the train comes back." He turned round towards the wood, as did his sister. And there, sitting on the tree stump right in front of them... was the owl. Sam started. His mouth opened wide as if to say something. But nothing came out. The children were silent, transfixed. The owl looked even bigger close up. He was enormous. Sitting on the tree stump he was taller than the children, his eyes like two setting suns.

"H-Hello," stuttered Sam. He was in awe of the huge bird right in front of him. The owl blinked lazily. It was difficult to tell if he was looking at them or through them. Close to, the children marvelled at the owl. His plumage was a hundred different shades of brown, barred and speckled, shimmering and glistering in the sunshine, from the deepest chocolate brown, through red brown and gold brown to brown so light it was almost the colour of cream. And his feet... they were huge, as big as a blacksmith's hands. But it was his eyes... they were so wide and bright. When the children looked at them (and they couldn't not look at them) they were spellbound, almost hypnotized. They couldn't look away.

"My, he's so beautiful," Samantha whispered to her brother, forgetting that the owl could easily hear the very slightest sound.

"Yes," said the owl, making a purposeful effort to stand up straight and puff out his feathers (which made him look even bigger), "you're quite right. Owls are, generally speaking, very beautiful and I'm forced to admit that, even for an owl, I'm particularly handsome. There's no sense in denying it, is there? That would be dishonest, wouldn't it?"

"Yes. I suppose it would," Samantha agreed. She thought – what a conceited bird! But knew better than to say so out loud for the owl would surely hear her.

"Do owls have names?" asked Sam.

"What do you think?" replied the owl.

"I'm sure they do," said Samantha confidently. The owl did not reply.

"What's your name?" asked Sam.

The owl remained silent.

"I'm called Sam."

"And I'm Samantha".

The owl seemed to be thinking. Presently he said, "Ee'boo." The children weren't sure if the owl had told them his name or just made a noise that owls make.

"He Bo," said Sam. "Is that your name?"

"No, no!" the owl said impatiently. "My name is Ee'boo."

"Ee'boo," Samantha repeated correctly.

Behind them the twins could hear the chugging of another steam train, this time coming in the opposite direction carrying full coal wagons to the junction. The twins turned round to see the familiar plume of white steam and smoke in the distance. They felt a draught of air against the back of their necks and turned round to the tree stump again. The owl had flown off. They could see his enormous wings slowly flapping as he flew into the wood, soon disappearing into the trees.

"Oh, he's gone," said Sam. "I wish he wouldn't keep flying off like that. I did want to talk with him. The train must have frightened him."

"I don't think he's the sort of person..." Samantha corrected herself. "...The sort of owl who is frightened of anything. He just seems to like... coming and going." Then she sighed. "But I wanted to talk with him too. I hope we will do, one day."

Chapter 3

First thing on Sunday morning, as usual, the twins would visit their Nan. Nan lived alone in Holly Cottage, a small, white-painted cottage on the edge of Dilhorne village. Then they would go to the wood to play before going home for a sumptuous Sunday dinner cooked by their mother. The children liked talking with Nan. She always had something interesting to tell them and usually a treat – an apple or an orange – or if they were very lucky a bar of chocolate.

As they approached Holly Cottage Samantha said to her brother, "You haven't told anyone about him, have you?" meaning the owl. "It's our secret. We don't want everyone to know. They'll all go to the wood and frighten him away."

"No," said Sam. "I haven't told anyone."

Expecting the children, Nan had left the back door on the latch. Sam pushed the door open and they went inside. Nan was at the kitchen sink. She turned and smiled at them. "There are some nice red apples in the bowl if you want one – I bought them at the market yesterday." The children ran into the front room. The fruit bowl was on the sideboard. The twins took an apple each. Samantha looked at the picture in the silver frame, which had pride of place in the centre of the sideboard, the face of a handsome, smiling young man. It was James, Nan's brother, who had been killed in the Great War when Nan was a little girl. Nan talked more about him than of anyone, how he had won a place at the grammar school, how he was going to be a teacher.

"These apples are huge," said Sam, taking a large bite from his apple. Samantha didn't reply. She was staring at the photo.

"What are you thinking about?"

"Oh, nothing," Samantha replied. In fact she was thinking how terrible it must have been for Nan to lose James. What would it be like if she were to lose Sam? She couldn't bear to think about it. Then Samantha turned to her brother and smiled. She

Chapter 4

T he children had had a wonderful week so far. Off
school and it was their birthday – what could
be better! Nan had taken them shopping to Longton
market one day. They had spent ages looking in
the pet shop window at the puppies and kittens, at
the terrapins swimming around in a glass tank,
and – best of all – at the handsome parrot sitting on
her perch, picking up Brazil nuts with her foot and
cracking them open effortlessly in her bill. Then they
had lemonade and cakes in a café. Another day Mum
had taken them for a picnic to Trentham Gardens
and they had been on the boating lake.

Most of the rest of the time they had spent in
Highwayman's Wood. Much to his sister's scolding,

Sam had been determined to climb as many trees as possible. Samantha enjoyed sitting down on the soft, dry, mossy ground making chains from the various flowers in bloom, daisies, buttercups and dandelions, which grew on the edge of the wood. All the days but one had been sunny. The one rainy day the children had stayed at home, reading. Sam read his book about King Arthur and his knights, Samantha her book about Black Beauty, which Mum and Dad had bought them for their birthday. The one disappointment was that, despite all the time spent in the wood, much searching and calling out "Ee'boo!", they had not seen the owl again.

At last it was Friday and there they were, standing by the signal at the railway where Barney had told them to wait. They leant against the fence, staring hard into the distance, looking for the first wisp of steam.

"I hope Barney hasn't forgotten," said an anxious Sam.

"He won't," said Samantha. As she spoke they heard a distant whistle, but it sounded different from Florence or Whiston or Hawarden, the locomotives they knew on the railway.

Then they saw the train, like none they had seen before on the railway, or anywhere else. It hauled majestically into view, slowed down and stopped beside them. In front was the most magnificent looking engine the twins had ever seen. Barney was on the footplate, beaming with pride. Harry was standing behind him looking just as proud. Like Florence, the loco had six wheels but it looked much older and much grander. The locomotive was painted a rich chestnut brown with glistening bands like gold around the boiler and cab panels. There was so much copper and brass, so highly polished it shone like more gold – round the top of the tall chimney, round the safety valves, round the cab windows, the handrails on the cab and boiler. The whole loco glistened in the sun, absolutely spotlessly clean, as if Barney and Harry had been polishing it every day for a year. The loco stood still, gently simmering away, sounding very pleased with itself, a wisp of steam from the safety valve. Sam looked at the nameplate on the side of the boiler. There were a lot of highly polished brass letters.

"Bel..." Sam tried to read out aloud. But he didn't get any further. There were too many letters – it was a very long name.

Behind the loco were two little passenger carriages. That was very unusual. The twins had never seen passenger carriages on the Foxfield

Railway before because the railway usually only carried coal. Just as Sam was captivated by the loco, Samantha was entranced by the carriages. They were perfect! They were painted chocolate brown with white panels around the windows and white roofs. The windows were lined out in red and gold paint. Just as on the loco, all the brasswork – door handles, handrails, door hinges – shone brightly in the sunshine.

"Like her?" shouted Barney.

"Yes!" the twins shouted back in chorus. Barney hopped down from the loco cab.

"Now," said Barney. "Ye mun never do this unless an adult tells thee, but climb over the fence... Here, I'll help thee." The two children scrambled over the fence with Barney assisting. Barney raised his hand and arm, in a grand gesture towards the loco.

"This is Bellerophon," he said. "Or Bel as I calls her for short." He lowered his arm, turned, and made the same gesture towards the carriages. "And these are the Kittens, as I calls 'em."

"Bel and the Kittens!" Samantha laughed. "I like those names!"

"You two get up into the cab – now stand well back and don't touch anything – it might be very hot. We don't want thee burning thee'selves on thee birthday!

I'll run round the carriages with the loco and we'll run down to Caverswall with the two of you on the footplate. Then we'll run back down to the colliery, with you travelling in the Kittens. First passengers they've carried in thirty years."

The children were, to be honest, a little frightened when they first went up into the loco cab. But not for long. Soon they felt very much at home. The cab was surprisingly high off the ground. When you were on it the loco seemed much bigger. There were pipes, brass wheels and levers everywhere. The fire, used to heat the water in the boiler to make steam, felt very hot whenever Harry opened the firebox door to shovel on more coal. With a toot on the whistle – so loud it made the twins jump – they were off to Caverswall. There was so much going on in the loco cab that the twins didn't really notice where they were along the line, Barney and Harry turning wheels one way, then the other, pulling levers, then pushing them back, shovelling coal and every now and then giving a toot on the whistle. As soon as the locomotive picked up speed it seemed to lurch and bang and sway all over the place so the twins hung on tightly to the handrail at the side of the cab.

"When I first started on't railway, more than thirty year ago, I found Bel and the Kittens at the back of a siding at Caverswall, unused and unwanted," Barney explained as they chugged along. "I thought to meself – what a shame. I could make summat of those. So I managed to get 'em into an old shed that wasn't used for anything. And over the years I did 'em up meself. A few hours after work each day, a few hours at weekend. My brother Lockwood used to come and help me. A few years ago, when Harry left school and started on't railway, he helped as well. And here they are now, better and brighter than they've ever been." Barney shook his head. "Ee, if you could have seen what a sorry state they were in before we started."

"So you've been working on them all that time – thirty years?" Sam asked. He couldn't believe anything could take that long.

"Aye thirty years," Barney replied. "And I wouldn't have missed a day of it."

The loco slowed as it came into the yard at Caverswall. The twins looked around. Sam was fascinated by it all. Samantha thought how untidy it looked. There were bits of locomotives lying all over the place – chimneys, wheels, boilers. Some looked very rusty. There were lots of wagons in sidings. There was a huge shed, with railway tracks leading into it. The twins could see men working on locos and wagons inside, banging and hammering. There was a big water tank on a tower – much bigger than the old one at Highwayman's Wood – and great piles of coal stacked up.

Bel and the Kittens came to a stop in the yard. Barney ran the loco round to the other end of the coaches. Then he and the twins got down from the cab (it looked even further to the ground on the way down) while Harry coupled up.

"Now we'll go back in style," said Barney. They walked to the first coach behind the engine. There were steps up to the door but it was still quite a way for the twins to get up. Barney guided the children so they did not slip or fall. They sat down inside the coach, Barney got in with them and clanged the door shut. The twins looked round, fascinated. They had been in railway carriages before – but not like these! Everything was made of wood or brass. The carriages were obviously very old but everything smelt very new. The smell of fresh paint, varnish and polish. The seats were of a light coloured polished wood (but surprisingly comfortable) while the inside carriage walls were of a darker wood. The brass door locks fascinated Sam as did the embossed leather straps used to raise and lower the windows.

"Will Harry be alright driving on his own?" asked

Samantha.

"Oh yes, he'll be fine," said Barney. "He's a good lad, young Harry, and the fire's well made up."

You got a much better view out of the carriages than from the loco and the ride was much smoother. On leaving the yard at Caverswall they first went through meadows with sheep and young lambs. Then the line curved to the left and went over a road crossing. Then the line turned right, then left, then right again. This time the fields were full of black and white cows. Next they went through a cluster of trees with a pool right beside the line. A large grey heron was standing motionless, on one leg, completely unconcerned by the train passing close by. The line straightened out and in the fields were more sheep and lambs and another meadow with two ponies. The children realised they were coming up to Highwayman's Wood, where they had got on the train. Going past the wood, the train slowed to a snail's pace. The line descended steeply towards the colliery, curving to the right as it did so, the flanges of the loco wheels grinding and squealing against the rails of the tight curves. The line straightened out as it passed the back garden of Nan's cottage and – after a gentle curve – entered the colliery yard. Harry brought the train to a gentle standstill.

Barney opened the carriage door and climbed down.

The twins were amazed at how much railway track there was at the colliery. There were sidings everywhere, dozens of coal wagons, some full, some empty. A pretty little locomotive, bright red with the number "2" on the cab side, was slowly pushing a string of wagon under a sort of bridge beneath a high building. Each wagon stopped beneath the bridge, there was a loud rumbling sound and a cloud of black dust gently drifted all around the wagon as coal was dropped into it from above. There were all sorts of buildings, set out higgledy piggledy across the site, some small, some very large. Many of them had steam coming out of pipes and chimneys. There were two enormous towers, each with a pair of great wheels at the top – like cartwheels but much bigger – and one of the pairs of wheels started spinning.

"Look yonder," said Barney pointing to the revolving wheels. "That's pulling up the cage from the bottom of the pit, full of coal just mined today. More than five hundred tons of coal are mined every day. It all has to come up that shaft. There'll be more than a hundred men underground right now hewing it out."

"Wow!" said Sam, always impressed by large figures. "Where does all the coal go?"

"Well," explained Barney, "it goes along the Foxfield Railway to the main line at Blythe Bridge. From there the trains take it all over Staffordshire and beyond. To the factories, the power stations to make electricity, to the gasworks to make gas, to the steelworks to make steel, to power the factories to make pots and pans, cars, bicycles... some of it you've burned in your own grate at home, I should think. We could never manage without coal, Sam." He added solemnly, "It powers the modern world. If you came back here a hundred years from now this colliery would still be producing coal. You mark my words."

"But why is it called Foxfield?" Sam asked. "Are there foxes in the field?"

"Aye, there are plenty of foxes in yon fields. And badgers, rabbits, hedgehogs as well. But it's not named after a fox. Or a field. It used to be called Dilhorne colliery but then all the miners began to call it Foxfield after a man they call Tom Foxfield."

"Did he build the colliery?" asked Sam.

"No," Barney explained. "He saved the lives of many men – dozens, hundreds maybe, miners trapped after an explosion and roof fall underground. It were nearly a hundred years ago it happened. He led them all out through a passageway that no one knew about and they were all saved. And the queer thing is..." Barney puffed on his pipe "...When they looked afterwards, nobody could find the passageway again. No one's ever found it to this day."

"Was Tom Foxfield a miner?" asked Samantha.

"No," said Barney. "He wasn't a miner. No one really knew who he was or how he came to be there that day. And it wasn't just not being able to find the escape tunnel afterwards that were queer. When the miners were describing 'owd Tom afterwards, they all described him as different. Some talked about a white man with grey hair. But others said it were a black man. There were even one or two who swore it wasn't a man at all, but a woman."

There was a sudden, loud, piercing whistle from one of the colliery buildings. The children could see steam coming out of the big brass whistle on the colliery office roof.

"That's the three o'clock shift change," said Barney. "Come on, you two. We don't want to be late for Mrs Pyke. Otherwise I'll be in trouble!"

Barney and the twins waved goodbye to Harry on Bel's footplate as they were getting ready to return to Caverswall. The three of them hurried down the colliery path to the gate leading to Whitehurst Lane.

"Is it a long way to walk to your house?" asked

Samantha.

"We're not walking," said Barney. "I told thee we'd travel in style today and we will. And it's not a house."

"Not a house?" said Sam. "What is it then?"

"Ah, thee'll see soon enough."

"I bet he lives in a railway carriage." Samantha giggled to her brother.

"I'm sure he does – it will be another one like the Kittens!"

As they came to the gate they looked to the right. There, parked under the shade of a tree, was a motorcycle and sidecar.

"There we are!" said Barney pointing to the three wheeled contraption. "Travel in style we will."

"Wow!" shouted Sam, bouncing up and down with excitement. "Fantastic!" He rushed up to the machine. Like everything Barney had, the machine was polished bright and spotless. The motorbike had gold painted mudguards and petrol tank, and on the side of the tank were the letters "BSA". Attached to the motorcycle was a gold painted sidecar, like a tiny canoe, a low perspex windscreen with two little seats, one in front of the other. Barney reached into the sidecar and pulled out his crash helmet, putting it on his head and doing up the strap beneath his chin.

"In thee get," said Barney.

The two children scrambled into the sidecar. It was surprisingly comfortable. Barney climbed on the motorcycle, fired up the engine (it sounded very loud), and off they went down the lane. It was very draughty travelling in the sidecar but on a hot day like this, it was quite pleasant. Travelling so low down everything looked different. The air rushing by seemed to intensify all the smells, the grass, the tarmac on the hot road, the petrol from the engine. Along they went. When Barney saw somebody he knew (and he seemed to know everybody) he'd give a toot on the horn and wave. The children waved too.

Along they went, lanes the children didn't recognise, this way and that, up and down hills. After what seemed like quite a long way they began to slow and Barney turned into a narrow track with a sign reading "Crooked Gate Farm". Sam leaned forward to Samantha sitting in front of him.

"Barney lives on a farm!" Sam said.

But just before they reached the farmhouse, Barney turned left, through the farmyard, scattering chickens and geese as the motorcycle trundled along, then through a wide gap in a high hawthorn hedge and into a meadow. Barney turned left and parked the motorcycle beside the hedge and switched off the engine. Everything suddenly sounded very quiet.

"Here we are," said Barney.

The children were puzzled. They were in a field parked beside a hedge. Where was Barney's house? Samantha turned round in her seat to ask this very question to her brother. As she did so she saw it, behind them.

"Look!" squealed Samantha. Sam looked over his shoulder and saw it too. The two children scrambled out of the sidecar. They stood and looked in amazement. Barney came up behind them and put a hand on each of their shoulders.

"Like it?" Barney asked.

"It's amazing!" said Samantha. "A boat – Barney lives on a boat!"

And indeed it was a boat, a canal narrow boat, raised on stout wooden blocks to keep it a few inches above the grass with a set of wooden steps leading up to the stern. The children hurried towards the handsome vessel and saw the name Sky Dancer painted on the prow. Mrs Pyke came out of the cabin and smiled at the children, wiping her hands on a towel.

"Hello children." Mrs Pyke smiled. "Ready for some cakes and lemonade? The cakes are just out of the oven!"

Chapter 5

The carpet of bluebells had long gone from Highwayman's Wood. It was now high summer and the sun was even hotter as the children had walked along the lane. But, reaching the wood they were now pleasantly cool and shaded beneath the high trees. Both children were wondering if they would see the owl today. Sometimes when they came here they did, but most times he wasn't there. Sam and Samantha walked slowly along. Sam had picked up a stick, which he was dragging along in the plants and bushes beside him.

"That was a lovely birthday party at Barney's house, wasn't it?" said Samantha.

"Yes," Sam agreed, "all those cakes. And the jelly!"

(Jelly was Sam's favourite.)

"She made all the biscuits herself. And the apple pie – that's my favourite. And the inside of the house – well, boat – was so pretty. So neat and tidy. All that lovely embroidery that Mrs Pyke has done. She's so clever."

Sam, to be honest, had not noticed the embroidery, fine though it undoubtedly was. "Do you know what I liked best?" he said.

"No."

"The ride on Barney's motorbike. That was fantastic! I want a motorbike when I grow up."

"No you don't," Samantha scolded. "Motorbikes are dangerous. You'd have an accident and hurt yourself."

"No I wouldn't," Sam protested.

"Fancy, though," said Samantha. "Barney said his boat's not been in the water for ten years!"

"Ten years – that's when we were born, ten years ago. But Barney did say he was going to get it back in the water soon, now it's all been properly repaired and painted. As soon as his brother's steam tractor is mended..."

"But didn't you hear what Mrs Pyke said? She said Barney had been saying that every year for as long as she can remember but they are still in the field!"

"Hmmnn," Sam grunted, adding hopefully, "I

think it will be soon now."

Sam was still dragging along his stick. It became tangled in some thick green leaves. They looked more closely at the plant. It had curious purple, round flowers, rather unpleasant looking, Samantha thought.

"I've never seen that plant before," said Sam. "I wonder what it is." He reached out towards the flower, intending to pick it for a closer look.

"Don't touch that," said a voice behind them. The children turned round. There was Ee'Boo sitting on a low branch.

"It's poisonous. You mustn't ever touch it or get it on your hands."

"But it's only a little flower," said Sam.

"Doesn't matter. There are many good things in this wood. But there are some bad things. It's important to know one from the other."

"What's it called?" asked Samantha. "I've never seen it before."

"Belladonna," came a quite different voice. "But your sort call it Deadly Nightshade."

The children turned round again. Both their mouths fell wide open in astonishment. There was a little grizzled man. Well, he looked like a man. But he was not quite as tall as Sam or Samantha even in his stout hobnail boots. He had a white beard and long white hair tied in a plait hanging down his back. In the plait were tied bows and ribbons of coloured cloth. He wore a dark green jerkin with blue breeches. Round his waist was a belt from which dangled all sorts of things, including a hammer, billycan and some rope. On his head was a battered tin helmet with a brass oil lamp on the front.

"May I introduce you to Zurfass?" said the owl, rather formally. "Zurfass, these are two friends of mine, Sam and Samantha." Zurfass bowed politely and the two children bowed back.

"You're not an owl, are you?" a confused Sam asked rather stupidly.

"No," Ee'boo confirmed. "Sadly, not everyone can be an owl. He's a Knocker, a mine-pixie."

"I've seen you two here before," said Zurfass. He spoke in a rasping, wheezy voice.

"Really?" said Sam. "We've never seen you."

"No," laughed Zurfass. "A Knocker keeps himself to himself if he can. Best way."

Although at first he seemed short of breath, and although he stood hunched forward rather than standing up straight (because of many years working in low, narrow tunnels underground) Zurfass could move very quickly and nimbly. He sprang across to a plant beside the Deadly Nightshade.

"Now see this," said Zurfass with a smile, "this is a lovely plant – Woodbine – can you smell its sweet smell?" Zurfass put his large nose to a collection of the cream-and-pink trumpet flowers which twined high up a bush and he breathed in deeply. "Beaut-i-ful!" he sighed. "On a warm summer's night you can smell it all through the wood. Butterflies love this plant. So do the little dormice. They drink the sap and use the stems to make their nest. And in the winter there are beautiful red berries for the birds to eat."

"Ugh," said Ee'Boo, "eating berries," and he gave a shudder.

"Woodbine?" asked a puzzled Sam. "That's a funny name for a plant. Those are the cigarettes my Dad smokes."

"Ugh!" said Ee'Boo again. "Cigarettes!" And he gave an even bigger shudder.

The pixie lay down on the soft, dry, springy forest floor. "Hmmnnn, very comfortable," he said, "very pleasant spot."

The children sat down on a log, talking with the pixie while the owl sat on a branch above them, taking it all in.

"Do you live in Highwayman's Wood?" Sam asked

the pixie.

"Not so much in it as under it," Zurfass replied. "We Knockers spend most of our time underground. But in the summer we do like to come up now and then for some fresh air in the shade of the trees."

"Do you mine coal?" asked Sam.

"No, not coal. What good is coal to us? We don't light fires. Why should we? All that nasty black smoke. Underground it's always warm, just as warm in the winter as in the summer. No need for coal fires. And we have our oil lamps for light."

"What do you mine then?" asked Samantha.

"Nice things, shiny things, pretty things," said Zurfass. "Silver, gold..."

"Silver and gold!" Sam said excitedly. "Is there silver and gold under Highwayman's Wood?"

"Oh yes," said the pixie. "But you'd never find it. But there are little bits here and there. And Knockers have a special nose for silver," Zurfass said, rather smugly, tapping his own impressive nose with his bony finger as he spoke. "And there are lots of lovely stones and rocks too. They polish up something wonderful."

"Are there many Knockers living here?" asked Samantha.

The pixie's face clouded over in a frown. "Not as

many as there were."

The two children sat talking with their new friend for quite some time. The owl – who was something of an old friend by now – was listening quietly from above but saying little himself. The pixie told them much about the wood, the flowers and all the creatures who lived there, about the Ranger, about how once there had been a great fire in the wood, about the coming of the gizaki, about the great storm which had blown down most of the trees in the wood, about the summer when the sun never shone, about so much. Things the children hadn't known. Things that no one else could have told them. Zurfass seemed to know a great deal about the wood for someone who spent most of his time underneath it. But, there again, he had been coming here for a very long time.

"Do you remember the Highwaymen?" Sam asked.

"Highwaymen?" Zurfass sounded puzzled. "What's that"?

"This is Highwayman's Wood – there must have been highwaymen – robbers with pistols and cloaks – they ride horses, wear masks and rob you!" Sam said excitedly.

"No, I never remember anyone like that," said the pixie, shaking his head. "I remember once gizaki did live here. They lived in wooden houses on big wooden wheels. They had horses. The horses pulled the wooden houses. They came one day, stayed a while, then left. They were always lighting fires," Zurfass added disapprovingly. "But no robbers with guns."

Sam was in a bit of a sulk as he walked home with his sister. How strange, he thought.

"Why on earth should this be named Highwayman's Wood if there were no highwaymen?" he asked Samantha. He sighed. "I wish things would be as they should be."

Chapter 6

The great day had arrived! Barney's boat was
going back to the canal at last! As the children
stood on the brow of the low hill they saw the whole
exciting scene before them. There was Lockwood
Pyke's steam traction engine, brilliantly turned out
in royal blue and black; it looked enormous! Clouds of
white steam were pouring from the tall chimney, the
huge flywheel on the side of the boiler was clattering
round. The twins hurried down the hill. A rope,
thicker than any Sam or Samantha had ever seen,
had been put all round Barney's boat. Wooden rollers,
like logs, had been laid on the ground in front of the
boat and the traction engine winch was pulling on
the rope so that the boat was gently, slowly, carefully

being pulled forward on to the logs so it moved as if on wheels. Two large beams had been set up leading onto a long trailer so as to make a gently sloping ramp. The children were right up by the traction engine now, fascinated. Besides Barney, his wife Cressida and his brother Lockwood, there were several other men helping out. Checking the position of the rope, signalling to push the boat a bit to the left or a bit to the right. A crowd of onlookers had gathered – where they came from in such a remote country area the children couldn't imagine – and everyone was enthralled by the spectacle.

Barney was rushing about here and there, shouting for people to be doing this and that, but none of the others were taking much notice. It was Lockwood, as always wearing his top hat, thumbs in the buttonholes of his open waistcoat, standing proudly beside the steam winch at the rear of his traction engine, who was clearly in charge. Cressida Pyke stood some way back, quite still, for a long time saying nothing, but observing events closely. Then she spoke:

"Barnabas Pyke – will you keep away and let them as knows what they're doing get on with it!" Cressida scolded her husband.

As the boat began to ascend the ramp, it trembled

slightly. "Mind you don't break my best crockery!" shouted Mrs Pyke, then mumbled something to herself. So very slowly, the boat was hauled up the ramp. Eventually, after what seemed a very long time, the boat was on the trailer. "See how much the trailer has sunk down with the weight of the boat!" said Sam. The great flywheel of the traction engine slowed and stopped. The plumes of steam from the chimney now became mere wisps, and all was suddenly quiet.

The workmen unfastened the rope from the winch and put large wooden wedges between the side of the boat and the trailer beneath. Then they took more ropes and lashed the boat down to the trailer along all its length. While all this was going on, Sam, fascinated by the traction engine, was watching Lockwood shovelling coal into the firebox of the traction engine. He could see bright orange flames through the firebox door and feel the heat even where he stood. Then Lockwood turned some brass wheels on, turned another off, then pulled a lever. He turned to Sam. Sam could see Lockwood's hands were filthy and there was a large smudge of soot across his face. Lockwood beamed "Plenty of steam!" he said to Sam.

"Boat's secure!" shouted one of the other men.

"Righto!" shouted Lockwood as loud as he could. "Mind out, everyone – we're off!" Lockwood proudly raised his top hat (which had a large peacock feather in it to mark this special day) to the eager crowd and sounded a long, loud blast on the whistle. The flywheel began to turn again, slowly at first, ever faster, and steam – mixed with black smoke this time – shot high out of the engine's chimney into the sky. The traction engine gave a shudder, then slowly began to move forward, hardly moving at all at first. Gradually it began to move more quickly, pulling the trailer and boat behind it. The crowd of people let out a great cheer and began to clap their hands and slap each other on the back. Sky Dancer was on her way home at last!

Chapter 7

"Hullo there!" came Zurfass's wheezy voice followed by a chuckle. "What have you two got planned for today?"

The children returned the greeting.

"Nothing planned really," said Sam.

"Our Nan's coming round for tea today so we thought we'd come to the wood to see you and Ee'boo first," said Samantha.

"Yes," said Sam. "See our friends."

The pixie chuckled again.

"Friends," he said, then his expression changed to a frown. "Friends," he repeated and shook his head. "It's not good to have gizaki as friends, I fear. They cause trouble. They tell lies. They steal things."

"What's gizaki?" asked Sam.

"I think we are," replied Samantha.

"Yes, you are," said Zurfass. "Just little ones though, who are not so bad."

"But we don't tell lies," said Samantha. "We don't steal."

"Have you never told a lie?" asked Zurfass.

"No," said Samantha. Never.

"Yes you have!" said Sam. "You told Mrs Dobbs yesterday that she looked very nice in her new hat, the one with all the feathers. But then after she'd gone you laughed and said she looked silly; you said she looked like a parrot was perched on her head."

"But that wasn't a lie," said Samantha. "I was just being polite."

"But we want to be friends," said Sam. "We thought you might tell us more stories like you did when we were with Ee'boo the other day. They were really good."

"Stories," Zurfass said. Then he smiled. "Yes, I am a good storyteller. I'm famous for it. Everyone wants to hear my stories!"

"Well," said Sam, "go on then."

"Yes," said Samantha, "tell us about the other pixies. Can we meet them?"

"Meet them?" Zurfass sounded surprised. "Well,

perhaps sometime. But not now. They're all busy working. In the mines or whatever else they do."

"What else do they do? Apart from being miners?" asked Sam.

"Now," said Zurfass. He sat down on the ground and made himself comfortable. The children did the same.

"Take my cousin Wimbleberry. He's very famous. He's an apothecary."

"What's that?" asked Sam.

"An apothecary is someone who makes medicines to make you better when you're poorly."

"How does he make the medicines?"

"Oh, that's a secret. His father was an apothecary too and he taught Wimbleberry all about it. Most of the medicines are made from plants, I think. Wimbleberry knows all about plants. He's taught me about them... but not how to make the medicines from them. That's his secret."

Zurfass scratched his chin.

"Then there's my sister Cherryfrost and my cousin Juniper Silverglimmer. Cherry makes the most wonderful clothes you've ever seen. She made these–" he touched his shirt and breeches– "and my best suit. Oh, my suit is sewn with thread of pure silver!"

Zurfass was becoming quite excited talking

about his talented family. "Now, Juniper, she makes jewellery. But what jewellery! She..." But Zurfass suddenly stopped. Then he said, "Listen!"

At first the children heard nothing. But then they heard the music. A mournful, mellow, reedy sound played on some sort of flute. Yet the tune itself was quite bright and jolly.

"Come!" said Zurfass springing to his feet. "I'll show you a true friend if you want one, a friend to every creature!" The three of them walked briskly towards the sound of the music. The children had to run to keep up with Zurfass. As they went over the little wooden bridge across the stream Zurfass stopped briefly.

"I made this," he said proudly, stamping on the bridge twice with his foot. But then he was off again. They came to a small clearing not far from Zurfass's bridge. There they saw a strangely dressed figure sitting on the trunk of a fallen tree. As they approached, the strange man stopped playing. He stood up gracefully and put his flute – or whatever the instrument was exactly – inside his long coat. As the two children and one pixie stood still, a little way in front of him, the strange man smiled broadly and bowed very low, making a dramatic sweeping gesture with his hand and arm as he did so. Then he stood up straight.

"I'm very pleased to meet you," the man said.

"And we're very pleased to meet you too," the two children replied courteously.

"Are you the Ranger?" asked Sam, remembering something Zurfass had once told him.

"Some call me that," the Ranger replied.

"Well, I'm Sam and this is my sister Samantha."

"Yes," said the Ranger.

Samantha studied the man intently. He was very tall and slim. He was dressed all in grey. His boots were the darkest grey, his long coat, open at the front, a much lighter shade of grey, his breeches and jerkin somewhere in between. All was grey apart from the band of his wide brimmed grey hat, his fine gloves and the man's amazing eyes. The gloves and hatband were an intense shade of green, as bright as the grey was dull, the most beautiful shade of green Samantha had ever seen, but not one she could describe because it wasn't like any green she had ever seen before. The man's eyes were blue, but so bright and sparkling that Samantha was drawn to them. It was if they had a light shining behind them, just like Ee'boo's orange eyes. Samantha couldn't work out if the man was young or old, or somewhere in between; it was impossible to tell from his face.

But it was an incredibly warm, friendly face and the man's smile wanted to make Samantha smile too. Which she did.

"What does a Ranger do?" asked Sam.

"Do?" The man seemed puzzled.

"He looks after the wood," Zurfass stated confidently, adding "and everything in it."

"Yes, I suppose I do," the Ranger laughed. "But it isn't just the wood I have to look after, there's so much else..." He shook his head wistfully, "...so much else."

The Ranger took a long wooden staff which had been leaning against a tree trunk. "Come!" he said. "There are some friends I have to see." He set off with enormously long strides so that the children – and even the pixie – had to run to keep up with him.

"Greetings, Captain!" the Ranger said to a magpie sitting on the branch of a tree. "And how's your lovely wife today?" The bird flew down, landing on the Ranger's shoulder as he strode by. The magpie seemed to whisper something in the Ranger's ear.

"Yes!" the Ranger said in response to whatever-it-was the magpie had told him. "Yes, I should say so." And the Ranger laughed heartily. The bird flew away about its business,

Soon they arrived at the pond. Keeping up with

the Ranger, the children – and the pixie – were quite out of breath. Sam wondered if the Ranger had come to see the ducks. But no, he strode past the pond to a mound of earth at the foot of an oak tree.

"Hello!" The Ranger tapped the ground twice with his staff. Almost at once a black-and-white face appeared from a burrow by a large tree root. It was a badger. The first badger Sam and Samantha had ever seen.

"I didn't know there were badgers here!" Samantha said to her brother.

"Good morning, Mrs Brock!" the Ranger continued. "I've come to enquire about that youngster of yours." As he spoke two smaller black-and-white faces of the badger's cubs appeared either side of their mother. From the conversation that followed the twins learned that one of Mrs Brock's cubs had been injured in a cruel farmer's snare. He had been rescued by the Ranger and thankfully was now on the mend. At least, this is what the twins learned from listening to what the Ranger said. The badger's conversation amounted to a series of snuffles and grunts, which the Ranger understood perfectly even though they meant nothing to the children.

"Well, that's wonderful news, Mrs Brock. Thank you for your time." The Ranger gave a little bow towards the badger who respectfully returned the gesture before disappearing back inside the set with her cubs.

"All in order here," the Ranger said. "Now I must go to Kingsley Moor where I fear there's mischief afoot. Goodbye!" The Ranger gave another little bow but – before the children had time to respond – he had turned on his heels and in two or three long strides he seemed to completely disappear into the trees. All was perfectly quiet.

"Where's Zurfass?" said Sam. The two children looked around but there was no one else there other than themselves. The pixie had disappeared too.

"Well, he might have said goodbye," said Samantha.

"Hummnn," grumbled Sam. "I've never known a place like this for coming and going. Everyone... everything suddenly appears when you're not expecting it. Then suddenly they disappear just the same. I wish they would stay so you can talk to them properly. Ask questions..." For there were indeed many questions Sam wanted to put to his fascinating new friends.

"Yes," Samantha agreed. "They seem to be busy with important things to do. At least the Ranger does."

"What do you think of him, then?" asked Sam as the two children walked slowly back towards the railway line. Clearly the tall man in grey had made a deep impression on the children.

"The Ranger, you mean?"

"Yes."

"He had the most amazing eyes. I've never seen such bright blue eyes. That's what I noticed most about him."

"Blue eyes? His eyes were brown. Very dark brown. Almost black. I noticed his eyes too. And they certainly weren't blue."

"Honestly, Sam, you're just being silly now," said Samantha, somewhat annoyed with her brother. "You never notice anything about people. You only notice motorbikes and steam engines and aeroplanes. Why do you have to say silly things like the Ranger has brown eyes when you know it's not true? You do things like that at all the time, just to try to be clever."

"No I don't" Sam protested. "Anyway, I bet he's a knight!" he said enthusiastically.

"Don't be silly again. He doesn't dress like a knight. And he doesn't have a horse. Anyway, there aren't any knights anymore."

"Aren't there?" Sam replied. "And there aren't any

owls that talk either? Or any pixies?"

Just for a moment Samantha was lost for a reply. For she knew what her brother meant. This was a strange place, Highwayman's Wood. A wonderful, welcoming, enchanted place. She thought about it for a short while.

"How lucky we are to be here," said Samantha.

"Yes," Sam agreed.

The children heard the sound of a steam whistle through the trees.

"Come on," said Sam. "Hurry up – the train's coming!" And the two children scurried off towards the railway line.

Chapter 8

"I wonder what he'll be like," Samantha said as she and Sam walked slowly along the lane towards Nan's cottage.

"Well," said Sam. "He'll be very old and... I think he'll be bald... and have a long white beard."

"A beard like Zurfass, you mean?"

"Yes, but without the bows and ribbons!"

The two children looked at each other and giggled.

The twins were going to meet their great-grandfather for the first time. Mum had told them Grandad – as Mum called him – had come to stay with Nan for a while as looking after his own home had become a bit too much for him and he needed to rest.

"So, he's Mum's grandad?" asked Sam.

"Yes," said Samantha.

"So he's our grandad too – I thought he was dead?"

"No," Samantha said. "He's not our grandad. He's our great grandfather."

"Well," said Sam, not at all sure how these things worked. "Is he Nan's grandad too?"

"Sam, don't be so silly! He's her father."

"Her father? Oh, I didn't realise," said a slightly surprised Sam.

Reaching the cottage, the twins went inside and were greeted by a smiling Nan. She took them through to the little front room where her father was sitting in an armchair by the fireplace. He wasn't bald and he didn't have a beard. Instead there was an elderly man, small and wiry, with a full head of hair which was still more black than grey, twinkling bright eyes with a hint of mischief in them.

"These are your great-grandchildren," Nan announced proudly.

"Well hello!" Grandad said cheerily. "My, you're so much taller than I'd expected!"

"We're ten now," said Sam proudly.

Grandad screwed up his eyes and said, "What's that I can see? Come over here, will you?"

The children went closer to Grandad. He reached

out to Sam's ear, then pulled back his hand. There was a bright shiny sixpence in his fingers.

"What are you doing with a sixpence in your ear?" asked Grandad before pressing it into Sam's hand.

Then Grandad reached out with his other hand to Samantha's ear and drew out another shiny sixpence.

"And you too!" he said, giving the coin to Samantha. "What a funny place to keep your money!"

Samantha laughed but Sam looked puzzled.

"How did you do that?" Sam asked. "I didn't have a sixpence in my ear, did I?"

"Well, where else could it have come from?" asked Grandad.

Sam looked at Samantha.

"It's magic!" she said. Both children burst out laughing and Grandad chuckled too.

Nan went into the kitchen to prepare dinner while Grandad kept the children amused with a series of magic tricks and games. Samantha thought – for such an old man – Grandad seemed very young. Though he stayed in the armchair while they were playing, she was amazed at how nimble were his fingers, how sharp were his eyes and how quick were his wits.

One trick greatly frustrated Sam. Grandad put a shilling in the palm of one of his hands, then closed both hands tight to make a fist.

"Which hand is the shilling in?" Grandad would ask. "If you can guess correctly, you can keep it for yourself." Whichever hand Sam pointed to – even though he had just seen Grandad put the coin there – was the wrong hand. Grandad would open his other hand and there would be the silver shilling. Sam was determined he would get it right but after trying for what seemed to be a hundred times, he never did. How did Grandad do it, Sam wondered.

As ever, Nan's Sunday dinner was fantastic. Roast beef, roast potatoes, Yorkshire pudding, parsnips, carrots, peas and gravy, followed by apple pie and custard. Afterwards Nan, Grandad and the twins sat in the front room listening to Grandad talk about his memories of Staffordshire when he was a young man, when he first came over from Ireland and found work as a miner at Foxfield colliery.

Sam wanted to know all about Grandad's time as a miner and all about the colliery. He really wanted to know if Grandad had met any Knockers down the mine. But he knew that Samantha was worried about telling anyone else about Zurfass in case they came to the wood and frightened him away.

"It was in 1894 when I came from the farm in Ireland to Staffordshire, to look for work. I'll never forget the boat across to Holyhead. We got caught in a dreadful storm. I was as sick as a dog."

"Did you come on your own?" asked Samantha.

"Yes, on my own. I was 19 years old. I'd never been away from home before. Never been out of my village. I didn't see my mother again for more than 20 years. And I never saw my father again. I didn't go home again to Ireland until my father died. I had to go back to run the farm for my mother. She was on her own when my father died. My brother John was in London and my brother Pat was in Canada."

"Not seeing your mother for all that time," said Samantha. "I can't imagine that."

"Travel wasn't so easy in those days. People didn't travel then like they do now. Do you know, this is the first time I've been back to England since I left in 1916." Grandad shook his head and looked down at the floor. "That was a bad, bad year. I lost James in July and three months later my father died."

"When you worked in the colliery," Sam asked, "did you see any Knockers?"

"Sam – don't be silly!" Samantha scolded.

"Ah, the little leprechauns!" Grandad smiled. "I never saw one. But I certainly heard them."

"What did you hear?" asked Sam excitedly.

"Well, we'd be working in a narrow tunnel with

our hammers and picks and you'd hear the Knockers through the wall, tap-tapping away. If you went 'tappety-tap-tap' they'd answer back with the same 'tappety-tap-tap'.

"Couldn't the tapping have been your friends working in another tunnel nearby?" asked Samantha. "Or an echo?"

"No," said Grandad. "The tunnels aren't like that, echoes aren't like that. Our tunnels spread out from the main shaft. You know exactly where all the tunnels run and when you're half a mile along a tunnel, you're nowhere near another one. It was the Knockers alright."

Grandad took a briar pipe from the table beside him, and a leather pouch full of tobacco, and began to carefully fill the pipe.

"No. I never saw a knocker but they used to come into our tunnels regularly. You had to be careful with your snap."

"What's snap?" asked Sam.

"Oh!" Grandad laughed. "Snap is what we called our food, our dinner. You had to keep a watch on it otherwise it would be gone. They'd sneak in and take it. It was the fruit they liked. They'd leave bread, never take cheese or meat, but they'd go for the apples or pears or plums if you had them."

"So they stole your food?" said Sam.

Grandad had filled his pipe and was now trying to light it. It took a lot of matches.

"No," Grandad said. "No, they didn't actually steal. They'd do a swap, or a trade as the miners called it. If they took your apple they'd leave a little piece of polished stone or something in its place. They didn't steal. It was an exchange."

Grandad put his hand in his pocket and took something out. It looked like a marble. He handed it to Sam. "There, that's what a Knocker left for me once."

Sam took the little round stone. It didn't look – or feel – quite like anything he'd ever seen before. For the most part the stone was brilliant white. But it had flecks of intensely bright colours in it, mainly blues and greens. It was perfectly spherical, like a glass marble but somehow felt very different. Much lighter – it hardly seemed to weigh anything – and it was highly polished so that the coloured specks glistened brightly as they reflected the light.

"Can I keep it?" asked Sam.

Grandad frowned slightly. "No, not now, Sam. I'd rather you gave it me back. I've had it in my pocket for 60 years, through thick and thin. I'd be lost without it, my lucky charm."

Sam handed the Knocker-stone back to Grandad who put it back in his pocket. By now Grandad's pipe was well alight, and Grandad puffed away. Samantha didn't like the smell of the smoke at all but Sam thought it was rather nice.

"I think I'll smoke a pipe when I grow up."

"Sam!" his sister grumbled. "No you won't!"

"They were lucky for us, the Knockers," Grandad continued after a while. "Mines are dangerous places, you take it from me, and the Knockers knew before us if there was going to be a roof fall or a gas pocket opened. You hoped they were in their own tunnel nearby because they'd tap out a warning: tap-tap-tap-tap. Four taps together. Always four taps. They'd keep repeating those four taps over and over, each time just a bit louder... and you knew to get out quick."

Chapter 9

The long summer was coming to an end. It had been the best summer the twins could remember (not that they could remember many). But three days ago there had been the most dreadful storm.

"Look," said Sam as the twins walked through Highwayman's Wood, "the leaves are changing."

"Yes," said his sister, "they're going yellow and brown... it's autumn... and the storm has brought down lots of leaves already."

"It's not warm, even though the sun's shining – it doesn't seem to have any warmth in it anymore." Just as Sam spoke there was a gust of wind which rustled through the trees and made some of the leaves fall from the boughs above, fluttering silently to the forest floor.

"Bbrrrr," said Samantha. "It's getting cold and we don't have our coats. Should we go back home for them?"

"No," Sam replied. "I'm not cold." He was really. But he didn't want to go home because he didn't want to miss the chance of seeing Zurfass and Ee'boo again. He had not seen either of them for a while. Sam need not have worried because – as they came up to Zurfass's bridge over the little stream – there was the pixie sitting on the bridge, his legs dangling over the edge. And there, perched on a branch overhanging the stream, was the owl. The four friends exchanged greetings and news. Sam told Zurfass about his great-grandfather and how he had worked at Foxfield colliery and his stories about the Knockers.

"Ah yes," Zurfass chuckled, "they never saw us but we always saw them!"

There was another chill gust. "The sky's darkening," said Ee'boo. "I fear we're in for another storm."

"The storm the other day was dreadful," said Samantha.

"It certainly was," said Ee'boo. "Not weather to fly in."

"Ho ho!" said Zurfass. "You should live underground like me. Never bothered by the wind or rain or snow down there!"

"It must be awfully dark though," said Samantha.

"No," said Zurfass. "We have lots of lamps."

"I can hear thunder," said Ee'boo, the owl's hearing allowing him to hear the distant noise the others couldn't.

But the next clap of thunder they all heard. It was so loud that even Ee'boo was startled and puffed out his feathers. Then there was the most almighty flash of lightning right beside them and a clap of thunder so loud the children could not believe it. The whole earth shook. The four of them all turned to where the lightning had struck the ground. Standing there was the Ranger.

"Go!" said the Ranger. "Go now! Zurfass, you go underground right now. Ee'boo – don't go to the water tower. Go to the old oak tree the far side of the pond and hide in the trunk. Go now!" Without a word the owl flew off, as best he could, struggling against the fierce wind which had suddenly blown up from nowhere. The Ranger turned to the children. "This is the storm you'll never see the like of again if you live to be a hundred. Go quickly to your grandmother's. You're needed there. But when you come to the crooked willow tree on the corner, don't go any further down the lane, cut across the field to the back gate of the cottage. Hurry!"

The twins turned and ran. They could barely keep on their feet because of the wind. They ran as quickly as they could. Out of the wood, on to the lane out of the shelter of the trees, the wind was even more fierce. The roar of the wind in the trees was terrifying. Broken branches, blown by the wind along the lane, as if hurled by some unseen giant. The rain was driving down now so hard that it hurt their faces. Both children were soaked to the skin. They scurried down the lane to the corner where stood the crooked willow tree, all the time struggling against the gale. Sam carried on.

"No!" shouted Samantha, barely able to catch her breath for the wind. "Remember what the Ranger told us – cut across the fields and go in the back way."

"But the cottage is just along the lane!" Sam protested.

"Do what the Ranger said – please, Sam."

Sam hesitated. He took a few steps down the lane, hesitated again then turned back and followed his sister over the stile into the field. In the open field the wind was even stronger, the rain drove down like needles, and one huge gust blew both children over on to their backs. They rolled over, scrambling up on their hands and knees. As they looked up, back towards the lane where they had just been, they saw a huge lime tree, as tall as any tree they had ever seen, slowly fall towards them. It seemed to fall so slowly at first, gathering speed as it fell. It fell across the lane where Sam had wanted to walk, landing with the loudest crash the children had ever heard, shaking the ground beneath them and smashing to splinters the stone walls either side of the lane. The top of the tree landed within a few feet of where the twins were lying. The air above the fallen tree was full of birds who had been sheltering in the boughs, fighting the wind, till they were able to find new shelter in a different tree. The twins picked themselves up. Sam was shaken by what he had seen. "See," said Samantha, "what would have happened to you if you'd gone down the lane – that's where you would have been when it came down!"

"How did the Ranger know?"

"I don't know," said Samantha. "But he did!"

The twins fought the wind across the rest of the field, sometimes on their hands and knees, through the back gate of Nan's cottage, in through the back door of the kitchen to safety from the wild storm. They stood in the kitchen, both quite out of breath, absolutely wet through so they were dripping water onto the tiled floor. It felt so warm in the kitchen but they were both shivering with cold. They went to the door leading to Nan's front room, opened it, and looked through. They were surprised to see Nan talking to Dr Holford. Nan looked worried. Dr Holford, normally so bright and cheerful, looked very serious. Nan turned to the twins.

"Dear me – the state of you both!" said Nan. "But thank God you're both back safe."

"What's the matter?" asked Samantha. "Why's the doctor here?"

"It's father – Grandad," said Nan. "He's very poorly. The doctor thinks an ulcer has burst in his tummy."

"I'm going to go to the post office and phone for an ambulance to take him to Hartshill Hospital," said the doctor.

"Come and let me dry you both," said Nan, "and warm you up with some hot soup."

The children had just started to eat their soup when Dr Holford arrived back at the front door. He was soaked right through.

"Well, I've called the ambulance but it will take a while to get here because the road at the far end of the village has flooded – the river has burst the bank and the footbridge has been swept away too. It will have to come the long way round, around the wood."

"It can't," shouted Sam. "A huge tree has come down across Whitehouse Lane – it can't come that way either!"

"Then the ambulance can't get to the village either way. Oh dear." Dr Holford frowned.

Everyone stood in silence for what seemed a very long time. Then Sam shouted: "I know! I know!"

Sam ran through the kitchen and out through the back door.

"Where on earth has he gone!" asked Nan despairingly. "In weather like this and all!"

"I don't know." Trying to think what she would have done, Samantha said, "I think he might be going to the post office to call out the fire brigade to move the fallen tree".

Dr Holford shook his head. "That's a good idea but they'll have so many calls in a storm like this that they may take a long time to get to us. Anyway, I'll go back down to the post office myself now and see what I can do to persuade them."

After the doctor had gone Samantha and her Nan went upstairs to sit with Grandad. He was asleep. They didn't wake him. They sat quietly. Samantha could see from his face he was in pain and he looked red and flushed. Samantha looked through the bedroom window. The wind and rain were definitely dying down. The storm would thankfully soon be over, she hoped, dying away as quickly as it had blown up. Then Grandad opened his eyes. Nan stroked him gently on the forehead.

"Is the ambulance here yet?" he asked.

"It will be here very soon," Nan said, not being entirely honest.

The old man soon fell asleep again. Samantha thought the minutes seemed to go by so slowly. Then, she heard the sound of the front door opening. She wondered if Sam had come back. But the sound of footsteps on the stairs were not Sam's. The bedroom door opened. It was Samantha's mother.

"How is he?" she asked.

Samantha's mother stayed a while, sitting on the edge of the bed, holding her grandfather's hand. She spoke softly to him. Grandad would open his eyes for a moment and smile but then close his eyes again and turn his head away. Presently, Samantha's mother kissed Grandad on the forehead, saying she had to go but would soon be back. Everything was quiet in the room again save for the sound of Grandad's deep, slow breathing.

Then, after what seemed the longest time she had ever waited for anything, Samantha and her Nan suddenly started at the sound of an extremely loud whistle from outside.

"What on earth was that?" asked Nan.

Then the whistle blew again. "Toot toot!"

Samantha rushed to the window. There, standing still on the railway line at the bottom of the garden were Bel and the Kittens.

"It's Bel and the Kittens! Sam has brought Bel and the Kittens to take Grandad to hospital!"

"Kittens?" asked a rather confused Nan. But Samantha didn't hear her. She raced downstairs.

Dr Holford was coming in through the front door. He shook his head. "There's no way the fire brigade can get here for hours." As he finished speaking Sam and Barney came in through the back door.

"Now then, Doctor," said Barney as cheerily as ever. "Where's yon patient? If someone can phone at post office to have ambulance waiting at Longton station we'll have the old fellow there in fifteen minutes."

"How?" asked a puzzled Dr Holford.

"By train of course." Barney said it as though it was the most obvious thing in the world.

"Wonderful!" smiled the doctor.

Barney and the doctor virtually carried Grandad down the stairs with Nan making sure he was wrapped up well in plenty of blankets and fussing all the time. Carefully through the garden, through the back gate to the railway line. Barney and the doctor – with the help of Harry Longbottom – lifted Grandad ever so carefully into the first carriage. The doctor stayed with Grandad, as did Nan, as the train gently set off up the bank towards Highwayman's Wood, on its way to the main line at Blythe Bridge and then to the station at Longton.

As Barney waved goodbye to the two children standing by the garden gate he shouted: "Now thee two, off to the post office straight away and phone and make sure that ambulance is waiting for us at Longton station. Mind you tell them Dr Holford sent thee!"

The two children ran all the way and the ambulance arrived just as Bel pulled in to platform 1 at Longton station.

Still out of breath walking home from the post office, Samantha said, "What a day!"

"Yes," her brother agreed. Then he stopped, only just realising the rain and wind had now stopped completely.

"Look at all the broken tree branches and all the pools of water," Samantha said. As she spoke, the sun suddenly appeared, the sunlight reflecting off the wet road. The two children looked at each other and burst out laughing. Then Samantha turned to face her brother.

"Sam," she said, "I'm so proud of you going to fetch Bel and the Kittens. I would never have thought of that. You've saved Grandad's life. We'd never have got him to hospital otherwise." She threw her arms round Sam and gave him a big kiss.

"Urr..." protested Sam. "Stop it. That's so sloppy!"

The two children burst out laughing again and walked to Nan's in the sunshine, splashing in the puddles along the way.

Chapter 10

"" **T**he Isendrakan," said Zurfass grumpily. "I'm
glad it's good for something."

"What's that?" asked Sam.

"The Isendrakan is what folk like Zurfass call the
steam train," Ee'boo explained.

The four friends were sitting by Zurfass's bridge
in Highwayman's Wood. Sam and Samantha
were telling the owl and the pixie about what had
happened after the great storm, about the fallen lime
tree, about Sam fetching Bel and the Kittens to take
Grandad to hospital.

"Why don't you like the train?" asked a puzzled
Sam. "It's fantastic!"

"It was much better before the Isendrakan came,"

Zurfass insisted. "Belching smoke and fire, making the earth beneath tremble, setting fire to the grass and bushes. And all made of isen – ugh!"

"What's isen?" asked Sam.

"Isen is iron," Ee'boo explained, ever knowledgeable. "That's what pixie and faerie folk call it. They regard iron as unlucky. They hate it, won't touch it or even go near it."

"But your hammer, your tools," said Sam, pointing to the hammer hanging from Zurfass's belt.

"Bronze," said Ee'boo. "Knockers use bronze, or brass, or pewter, but never iron."

"And silver and gold." Zurfass added enthusiastically.

"Oh yes," Ee'boo agreed, "they certainly like silver and gold."

"Isen is for gizaki," said Zurfass, with a painful-looking frown. "Not for folk like us."

"And how is your great-grandfather now?" enquired the owl.

"Much better, thank you," said Samantha. "Since his operation he's sitting up now and eating his dinner. But he's still in hospital. I hope he'll be coming home soon."

"What's an operation?" asked the pixie.

"That's when the doctor cuts open your belly!" Sam

replied enthusiastically.

Zurfass recoiled visibly.

"Well, I don't like the sound of that," he said. "Gizaki are so strange. Why didn't you call the apothecary?"

"I don't know," said Sam uncertainly. "I don't think we know one."

"My cousin Wimbleberry is a brilliant apothecary. The best! He can make anybody better with his medicines and potions!"

But Sam was thinking about something Zurfass has said a little while ago. About things being better before the railway came.

"So you remember before there was a railway?"

"Of course," Zurfass replied.

"You must be very old then."

"Not at all!" Zurfass protested. "I'm one of the youngest Knockers round here."

"Have any children played in the wood before us?" asked Samantha.

"Very few," said the owl.

"There was just one." Zurfass smiled. "A little girl. She was the only one who ever came here regularly."

"Did you know her?"

"Oh yes," said the pixie. "I knew her quite well. It was many summers ago. She came here all the time.

Always on her own."

The twins could see that Zurfass was thinking.

"Very pleasant she was. Always wore a neat pale blue dress with a white collar. She had yellow hair – the colour of the morning sun, like yours – tied back with a blue band." Zurfass sighed. "And one day she just stopped coming. She never said goodbye but she never came back again."

"Do you know her name?" asked Samantha excitedly.

"Of course," said the pixie. Her name was–"

"–Alice," said the owl.

"So you knew her too! That's our Nan, our grandmother!"

"No," said Zurfass. She can't be your grandmother. She's just a little girl, barely older than you."

"Not any more, I fear." The owl sighed. "I've told you before, Zurfass Blatherstone, you know so little about gizaki. They change."

Ee'boo shook his head in dismay. "They do it all the time. I don't know why. It's so very tiresome of them. You never know where you are with them. They keep changing what they say, they keep changing how they look. Alice was a very polite young girl. She knew all about the animals, the birds, the flowers and the trees. I too was surprised when she suddenly stopped coming here. But with gizaki, well, I don't suppose you can expect anything else."

"We won't stop coming here. We'll come here forever," said Sam.

"Ah, but you will stop coming," said the wise old owl. "You mark my words."

Zurfass continued to appear deep in thought.

"Stay here," he said. "I'll be back in a few moments."

They watched the little figure in blue and green walking into the trees and out of sight.

"I wonder where he's gone," said Samantha.

In a short while Zurfass returned. As he grew near they could see he had something shiny in his hand. He came up to the twins and handed something to Samantha. It was a locket, made of silver, hanging from a silver chain. She had never seen anything so bright and shiny, which sparkled so much.

"It's beautiful!" said Samantha. She held the locket in her right hand, stretching the chain out with her other hand. It was surprisingly heavy for such a small thing.

"I think it belongs to your grandmother, to Alice. I've taken good care of it. Polished it every day." Zurfass smiled proudly. "The chain had broken and I mended it."

Sam came close and peered at the locket. Samantha carefully opened it up, looking at the tiny black and white photo in the locket frame. Though the photo was small it was very clear. It was of a smiling, handsome young man wearing a soldier's cap.

"That's our great uncle," said Samantha. "Nan's brother James. He was killed in the Great War when Nan was a little girl. Nan will be so pleased to see this."

"How did you get it?" asked Sam.

"It was many summers ago," said Zurfass. "I was walking along – just over there, in fact – and I saw something hanging from the leaf of a fern, something bright and shiny. I went over and this was it." He pointed to the locket. "I thought it might belong to the little girl. I thought she might have dropped it. So I picked it up to keep it safe for her. But she never came back. She just stopped coming here."

"Thank you, Zurfass, for taking such great care of Nan's locket," said Samantha. "She'll be so very pleased when I give it back to her. She won't believe it! Thank you both so very much!"

"Yes, thank you," said Sam.

"And do give Alice – your grandmother, I mean –

my very best regards," said Ee'boo.

"Mine too," said the pixie.

Chapter 11

Though the sun was shining it had no warmth at all so late in the year. Sam and Samantha had their coats on as they walked down the lane leading to Nan's house. The summer had been magnificent. But another summer had passed; the season had changed. The sun was no longer rising so high in the sky, so it seemed to shine on you from the side rather than from above. The children went through the back door of Nan's cottage into the kitchen. Nan was standing by the sink. She greeted the children with a smile and the children took off their coats and hung them up. As Samantha entered the kitchen she felt inside the pocket of her pinafore dress for her hanky and something wrapped inside it. It was there.

It was safe.

"Sit down at the table," said Nan. "I've made some iced buns for you." The children sat down. Nan was surprised, as she sat down at the table herself, because rather than immediately taking a cake as they usually did, the children just sat there looking at her.

"Are you not hungry today?" Nan asked. Sam and Samantha looked at each other. Then they looked back at Nan.

"We've brought a present for you," said Samantha. She reached inside her pocket and brought out her best lace hanky in which she had wrapped the locket.

"A present?" Nan sounded surprised. "But it's not my birthday."

"We think you'll like it," said Sam.

The children watched as Nan lay the little bundle on the table in front of her and opened the hanky. There, in front of her, was the locket and chain, as bright and as shiny as ever. The children watched their grandmother's face. It seemed to be frozen, expressionless, for ages, staring down at the locket.

"I can't believe it! I really can't," said Nan "Where did you find it? This is impossible! I lost it forty years ago!" Nan looked at Samantha, then at Sam. The children could see tears in their grandmother's eyes.

"Zurfass," Nan said. "Zurfass has kept it for me. I knew he would if he found it. Even though I didn't think I would ever see it again, I knew he would keep it safe for me." Nan looked at the twins. "So you know Zurfass?"

"Yes," said Sam. "He mended the chain for you. It was broken."

Nan looked at the tiny photo framed in the silver locket, the handsome young soldier.

"Do you know," she said, "that's the only photo of my brother James in his soldier's uniform. We have others of him, but this is the only one as a soldier. James gave this to me on the day he left for France. I never saw him again."

"Why didn't you tell us about Zurfass?" asked Samantha.

"Because you wouldn't have believed me, would you?" replied Nan. "Anyway, as time went by, all those years, I wasn't really sure if it had all happened, in the wood, Zurfass, and the rest of them. As you grow older, things seem different. There again–" Nan smiled– "You didn't tell me about him either, did you? But I always suspected, all that time you spend in the wood."

"And why did you go away after you lost the locket?" asked Samantha. "Why didn't you go back and look for it?"

"I'd gone to the wood that day to say goodbye, the day I lost the locket. I knew I couldn't go back to the wood for a long time because we were about to move away. My father – Grandad as you know him – had to go back to Ireland to look after the family farm after his own father died. We didn't come back here for a long time. Not until I was grown up and married myself when your own grandfather – my husband Jack – got a job at Foxfield colliery. He was very lucky to get it. There were very few jobs anywhere in those days – not like now – and families had to move about to find work."

"You know the owl too," said Sam. "He sends his... now, what was it... something like fireguards."

"His regards," Samantha corrected her brother. "He sends his best regards. Zurfass too."

"Dear Ee'boo!" said Nan. "Is he still as proud and conceited as he used to be?"

"He certainly is," said Samantha.

"But he's very clever, very wise," said Nan. "Ee'boo can tell you the answer to so many questions. That is, if he wants to." Nan reached up to put the locket chain round her neck. Samantha stood up and went round to help her fasten it.

"So, dear Ee'boo and dear Zurfass," said Nan.

"You know them both. Just fancy that! And do you know Wake Robyn, Wimbleberry Wagstaff and Tom Greyskins?"

"Who?" asked the twins together, sounding quite startled.

"So, you've not met them yet," laughed Nan. "I'm sure you soon will!"

– the end –

Foxfield Railway Stories

If you have enjoyed reading this book please look out for future publications in the series including *Wimbleberry Wagstaff, Sky Dancer* and *The Green Children.*

www.foxfieldrailway.co.uk